SPROUT AND THE HELICOPTER

"Sprout has an imagination, a sturdy determination, and a seemingly endless ability to land on his feet that will bring chuckles..." A.L.A. *Booklist*

Sprout loved holidays at the seaside. It meant extra helpings at mealtimes and lots of ice cream on the beach. But there was one thing which was becoming even more important to him than food: his ambition to own a rubber dinghy.

Just such a boat is being offered in the Regatta Week competition and Sprout is determined to win. And with only one day to go, he sets about it with a singleness of purpose completely in character. But it doesn't work out quite as he expects!

This delightful holiday story is the fourth one about Sprout, that engaging, and at times exasperating, small boy. His adventures this time lead him to make some new friends with the most unexpected people—and to find that even a disaster can have a happy ending.

Books by Jenifer Wayne

Sprout
Sprout's Window Cleaner
Sprout and the Dogsitter

Weekly Reader Children's Book Club presents

SPROUT AND THE HELICOPTER

Jenifer Wayne

Illustrated by Gail Owens

McGraw-Hill Book Company
New York   St. Louis   San Francisco

1 2 3 4 5 M U B P 7 8 9 8 7

Library of Congress Cataloging in Publication Data
Wayne, Jenifer.
  Sprout and the helicopter.

  SUMMARY: The desire to own a rubber dinghy ignites
Sprout's characteristically strong sense of purpose.
  [1.   Boats and boating—Fiction]   I.   Owens, Gail.
II.   Title.
PZ7.W35128Soh   [Fic]   76-56111
ISBN 0-07-068698-X lib. bdg.

SPROUT
AND THE
HELICOPTER

1

"Strawberry, please," said Sprout.

The ice-cream man grinned and scooped a generous helping of strawberry into a cone.

"Don't know where you put it all." He glanced down at the top of Sprout's bathing trunks. "Good thing they're stretch ones, eh? Your friend want strawberry, too?"

"No, thank you," said Raymond. "I won't have one at all. It's too cold."

"Baby," said Sprout between licks, and flapped back to the beach in his frogman's flippers.

"I can't help it, I'm not like you," Raymond muttered as he trailed along behind.

He had never said a truer thing.

Sprout was short, broad, and pink; Raymond was wiry, skinny, and brown. Sprout had always lived in London; Raymond had spent his first five years in Burma, where he said the sea was *warm*. He had never been to an English seaside place before.

But, although he shivered so much, once he got into the water he could swim like a fish. Sprout could still only splutter and splash and pretend.

"You've got one foot on the bottom!" Raymond would shout.

"I haven't!" Sprout would yell back; but as soon as he lifted his foot, he sank. All the same, he did come out of the water warm and hungry, whereas Raymond was just the opposite.

The only certain thing they had in common was that they were both seven and went to the same school.

They also lived on the same road. This was how they had come to be friends, and how Sprout's mother had grown rather sorry for Raymond. For one thing, he was so thin and hardly ate anything — an alarming sign for anyone who was used to Sprout. Then, Raymond lived alone with his mother in a top apartment, and hadn't even a little sister or a dog to liven things up. Sprout's sister Tilly was only three and often a nuisance to Sprout — but at least she was someone for him to "push around," as his father put it. Not that Tilly needed much pushing; she had a great gift for falling over, anyway. In fact, if there was an accident to be had, Tilly would be sure to have it. "Never a dull moment," their mother would sigh through the howls.

But Raymond must have had many dull moments up there in that apartment with a mother who suffered from headaches and said she "didn't think she could face" taking him away for a vacation.

So he had come to the shore with Sprout.

They were staying at Mrs. Lupin's, where Sprout's family had spent two weeks every year since he was in his carriage. Sprout liked Mrs. Lupin. She had told the big bouncing Irish maid, Eileen, always to ask him if he wanted "seconds," particularly if it was frankfurters or apple pie.

Eileen had been there ever since he could remember, too, and he had learned to understand her Irish brogue, which never changed, though the color of her hair did.

"Come on, now," Eileen would say, "only three pieces — you'll fade away!"

And she would dish him out a fourth piece of bacon and tweak the tuft of hair that had given Sprout his name.

But Eileen couldn't get used to Raymond. He worried her.

"He needs building up," she would say; but she

rightly suspected that if she pushed a second piece of lemon meringue pie in front of him, it would get passed on to Sprout when her back was turned. Sprout called it his thirds.

Mrs. Lupin had several elderly residents who sat at the same tables in the dining room, year in and year out. There was old Mrs. Court by the window, who never had the soup. There was Commander Piper by the door, with his own electric toaster, brown bread, and little bottle of pills.

Mrs. Lupin liked it when Sprout's family arrived; she said they livened things up.

But this year, there was one snag. Its name was Chops.

Chops was an Old English sheepdog that Sprout had found, lost in the snow. He had been allowed to keep it. Since then, they had become inseparable. Sprout had even insisted that Chops should sleep in his bedroom. When his mother protested, he reminded her of the noise Chops made at night if they left him in the kitchen alone. As soon as the door was shut, he would lift up his great woolly face and howl. In the end, Sprout used him for a bedside rug, and in the morning Chops would lovingly lick his face. Sprout thought it was very silly that he was made to wash in the bathroom as well.

So he was horrified when his parents said that while they were all at Mrs. Lupin's, Chops would have to go to a kennel. Sprout even said that in that case, he didn't want to go to the shore at all; he would go to a kennel himself. He was so firm about this, with his mouth so tight and turned down at the corners, that Tilly began to join in the fuss.

"Chops wants to go to the shore!" she wailed. "It's not fair!"

"No, it's not," said Sprout, and Tilly was so pleased to find him agreeing with her for once that she wailed even louder to oblige him.

What with her wailing, and Sprout's red-faced, tight-mouthed determination, their parents gave in. Chops went to the shore.

When Mrs. Lupin saw him, she actually looked quite put out, which was most unusual for her.

"You didn't say what kind of dog," she said. "I thought perhaps a scottie, or a poodle . . ."

"Holy saints!" shrieked Eileen, who had come into the hall to greet them. "Is it a polar bear you're bringing?"

"It's Chops," said Sprout.

Chops looked up at Eileen with his eyes showing like tiny bits of coal through his woolly mass of face.

"He's smiling!" said Tilly.

"He's hungry," said Sprout.

"Bless his heart!" said Eileen happily. There was nothing she liked better than feeding people, and it was clear that she would soon become as fond of Chops as she was of Sprout.

The snag was that Chops took up so much room. In

the lounge, where the visitors watched TV, he had only to stand up for the whole screen to be blotted out. Old Mrs. Court got more confused than ever over the weekly thriller, and Commander Piper missed a boundary and a catch in cricket. This irritated him very much.

After two days, Mrs. Lupin came to Sprout's parents in great distress and said she was afraid Chops would have to be kept out of the lounge; there had been complaints. She was truly sorry, because she didn't want to make Sprout or Tilly unhappy. But Sprout took it surprisingly well.

"If Chops can't watch TV, I won't," he said. "Can we stay in the kitchen?"

He knew that if Eileen was out there, Chops would get plenty of scraps, and he himself would be allowed to scrape out bowls, finish up the crumbs on the fruitcake plate, and even sometimes look for lumps in the jar of soft brown sugar.

"Well, as long as he's on a leash," said Mrs. Lupin rather doubtfully. "There are bound to be things on the table sometimes, and . . ."

But Sprout had gone to the kitchen.

"He doesn't waste words, does he?" Mrs. Lupin grinned at Sprout's mother.

Certainly, when Sprout did speak, it was always to the point; and he didn't talk unless he had to. He didn't see any sense in it. Besides, he was always too busy either eating or doing things.

He and Raymond sat on opposite sides of the

kitchen table, with Chops lying contentedly by the stove, and discussed the next thing that Sprout was determined to do.

Win a rubber dinghy.

The idea had started that morning, on the beach.

"Programs! Programs! Programs!"

A figure in a long flowered skirt approached them, ringing a hand bell. Another figure, in baggy clown's trousers, followed behind, carrying a sheaf of yellow papers. Both figures had huge, hideous, painted and varnished heads. Tilly was so much alarmed by these that she began, as usual, to howl. Whereupon the figure in the dress took off its head and turned out to be just a freckled, friendly, grinning boy.

"It's all right," he said. "We're only collecting for Regatta Week. Buy a program?"

Their mother bought one, just to keep Tilly quiet. She asked the trousered figure to take off its head, too, and underneath there was a rather pretty girl. Tilly's mouth fell open in mid-howl.

"Oh, she's cute, isn't she?" said the girl. "She ought to go in for the Costume Competition. You'll see it all in the program."

They put on their heads again and went off. Sprout thought it was silly to call Tilly cute; after all, she couldn't even read the program. He and Raymond pored over it. It announced that this was Seabay Regatta Week — and then Sprout spotted the Win-a-Dinghy Competition.

Now of all things in the world that Sprout wanted

this year, a rubber dinghy was at the top of the list.
Last year, it had been the frogman's flippers, and he
had managed to talk his parents into getting them for
him. But on dinghies he knew they were adamant: his
father mainly because of the expense, his mother
because of the danger. Sprout still went about in the
flippers, but they had lost their first charm. Mean-

while, he had seen hundreds of people floating around the water in rubber dinghies, some of them even eating ice cream as they bobbed up and down, and this seemed to Sprout the very height of bliss.

And now here was this competition.

"All you have to do" the program said, "is say what's wrong in the windows of any Seabay shop that is marked with a red spot. There are ten of these shops, including Trotter's Sports Store, where the prize dinghy is on display."

"Boy!" said Sprout. "Let's go and look at it!"

"What are the rules?" Raymond was always cautious. But then, "Hey!" he said, "I saw a dead fly in the baker's this morning!"

"What's the good of that?"

"Well, it's wrong for a fly to be on a bun, isn't it? And dead's worse."

"That doesn't count. They didn't put it there on purpose."

"How d'you know?"

Sprout ignored this silly question.

"Anyway, don't come if you don't want to," he said, and flapped off.

But by that evening, when they were both sitting at the kitchen table with Chops, Raymond had become really infected with Sprout's enthusiasm. It was very difficult not to be.

"Look, I've got four already," said Sprout, and his tuft of hair stood up like a piece of frayed rope. "The chocolate drop on the teapot, that was the first. That was clever, because it's a brown teapot, and they've put the chocolate drop so that it just fits on the lid knob. Anyway —"

"What shop?" asked Raymond. He had the yellow leaflet in front of him, with the list of names and blank spaces.

"Hardware store," said Sprout.

"It doesn't list any hardware stores."

"Let me look. Silly, here it is: Pooks, Hardware. That's what I said."

"You didn't, you said—"

"Oh, shut up and write it in."

"What shall I write?" Raymond had a pen poised.

"Chocolate drop on teapot, of course," said Sprout. He was sometimes amazed that Raymond, who was so good at arithmetic, could be so slow at other things. But Raymond's handwriting was neater than his, so he had given in about who should fill in the form. This was probably one of the things that had made Raymond keen on the whole idea; he loved filling in forms.

"All right. Next. Coal shop. I saw a blackberry in the middle of a little dish of coal. That was good, too, because blackberries are —"

"You always see food," said Raymond.

"Food!" exclaimed Eileen. "Here — catch!"

She threw Raymond a doughnut; it worried her to see a boy look so thin and serious.

"I don't really want one," he said, and wrote "blackberry" in the coal merchant's space.

"We're doing a secret," said Sprout. He took the doughnut.

"Oh well," shrugged Eileen cheerfully, "if it's secrets, I won't butt in." And she went to put the coffee cups in the sink.

"What else?" whispered Raymond. "You said four."

"Button in the fish shop," whispered Sprout.

"Button?"

"Yes. It was put on a fish, to look like its eye, but it was a button."

"They must have to keep changing it," said Raymond, "when that fish is sold."

"What's it matter?" Sprout said impatiently. "Come on, where's the fish shop?"

Together they found it on the list, and Raymond wrote "button" though at first he put in only one "t." Sprout was rather cross about this; his own spelling was quite good, and now Raymond had made a mess.

"I haven't! And anyway," Raymond added craftily, "they might be more likely to give us the prize if they think we're young."

Sprout was somewhat impressed with this, but he merely said:

"Anyway, hat shop. Caterpillar."

"*Caterpillar?* You wouldn't let me have fly, so why should you have caterpillar?"

"It was a joke one," said Sprout. "I've seen them in the toy shop. And they put it right in the middle of a bunch of flowers on a lady's hat. And it doesn't move. It can't."

"There's no hat shop on this list," said Raymond. He frowned at the paper.

"There must be. The shop had a red spot on it. *And* the caterpillar."

But search as they would, they could find no mention of a hat shop. Sprout looked so upset that Eileen said:

"You don't seem to be having much fun with those secrets. Looks more like you were taking a test."

"We are, sort of," said Raymond. "Hey," he whispered to Sprout, "shall we tell her? She might be able to help."

Sprout looked cautiously at Eileen. He knew that she had quite often gotten him out of trouble before and he trusted her.

So they told Eileen about the Win-a-Dinghy Competition and their present difficulty.

She got them out of that one immediately.

"Why here it is, right at the top: Darling's, the Milliners. 'Darling!'" she exploded. "She's as sour an old trout as you'll ever see!" And she explained that "milliner" was a rather old-fashioned word for "hat shop."

"But why does it all have to be such a secret?" she asked.

"My Mom and Dad," said Sprout. "They're against dinghies."

"But if we won it, they couldn't very well do anything," Raymond said.

"Fair enough," Eileen agreed. "Well, the best of luck!"

"Thank you," beamed Sprout. "You can have a ride in it when we win."

"'When'?" repeated Eileen. "Aren't you the opti-

mist! But what about *when* you have to send in this list. What about that?"

Sprout and Raymond had been so busy putting in "wrong" things that they hadn't bothered to read the small print at the bottom of the paper.

"Latest time for entries, Tuesday 8 p.m. No entry will be accepted after that—so HURRY!" Only the last word was big.

"My goodness, and it's Monday night now!" said Eileen. "You'll have to be snappy!"

"Oh, that's easy," said Sprout. "I got four in one morning."

"Maybe they were the easiest ones," Raymond said. He often said gloomy things.

Sprout glared at him.

"I want to win it," he said, and asked Eileen for another doughnut. If he had any doubt, he wasn't going to show them.

"After all," he reminded Raymond later, when they were in bed, "we've got a whole day."

"That depends," said Raymond.

"What d'you mean, it depends?"

"I think I've got a cold coming on."

Sprout grunted disgustedly. He knew that Raymond's mother had sent him off with all sorts of instructions about wearing sweaters and scarves. Sprout thought she was a silly fusspot.

"Anyway," he said, "if you can't come, I'll have to do it by myself, that's all. Only I might not let you have a ride when I get it."

Raymond grunted and went to sleep.

This made Sprout feel more determined than ever.

"You'll help, won't you, Chops?" he muttered, putting out his hand to the great woolly head beside his bed. Chops licked him, which of course meant "Yes."

2

But on Tuesday morning, there was every sign that Raymond's gloomy outlook might have good cause.

For one thing, it was raining.

"Well, nobody'll be able to go out this morning," said Sprout's father at breakfast.

Raymond sneezed.

"It doesn't sound as if you'd better go out anyway," said Sprout's mother. She also had received strict instructions about Raymond's health. "Nevermind, Sprout'll keep you company."

Sprout's heart sank. It sank so much that his mother's next remark was almost more than he could stand.

"Still, better today than tomorrow. That's when the Chads are coming down for the day. It'd be a shame if it wasn't fine for them."

"The *Chads*?"

"Yes, why not? There's a card from Mrs. Chad here. She says there's a day excursion, so she thought she'd bring Albina. Won't that be nice?"

"No," said Sprout.

"Oh, Sprout, don't be so mean! I'm sure a breath of sea air will do Albina a world of good. She's been looking paler than ever lately."

"Why can't they go somewhere else?" asked Sprout. It wasn't that he was really mean. Ordinarily, he would have put up with Albina, whose name rhymed with China; and he liked Mrs. Chad, who was fat and jolly and always had a few spare caramels in her apron pocket. But to look out at that blinding rain and to be told that it was a shame if it wasn't fine for the Chads tomorrow—that was too much!

"I hate Albina," announced Sprout. "She's stupid."

"She's not!" Tilly piped up. "She gave me a yo-yo!"

"Only because she couldn't work it herself," Sprout muttered.

Raymond sneezed again, twice. Eileen brought some more butter and gave Sprout a despairing and sympathetic look. The rain blew against the dining-room window in sheets.

"What's wrong with the Chads, anyway?" asked Raymond after breakfast.

"Nothing. I'm just fed up."

"Well, that's not their fault."

Sprout's mouth went tighter and straighter than ever; Raymond had a most depressing way of being right.

Mrs. Chad was very large; Albina, her daughter, was very small. Two years older than Sprout, she was still only about half his size. Mrs. Chad had been doing bits of floor-cleaning and baby-sitting for Sprout's mother ever since he could remember. She always brought Albina with her, so the Chads had become almost part of the family. Even when Albina was old enough to go to school, she was generally not well enough; so along she came with Mom. Since Sprout himself had been at school, he had not seen so much of them. When he did, he got along very well with Mrs. Chad, and he put up with Albina as he might have put up with spinach, or very thin soup.

But now . . .

The rain went on, with unbelievable slanting violence. Sprout's father said, "Well, that's that for this morning," and his mother told him to go and play with Raymond upstairs. Tilly pestered her mother to teach her Chutes and Ladders in the lounge; Raymond kept

sneezing; and Commander Piper tapped the barometer and announced that it would probably be a better
day tomorrow.

"Tomorrow!" thought Sprout. "What's the good of
tomorrow?"

And then there was more trouble.

"Oh no! I don't believe it!" Eileen shrieked.

Chops slunk out into the hall.

"Four brownies he's eaten!" she yelled. "Four!
And one of them without nuts, especially for Commander Piper!"

"He can have mine," said Raymond at once.

"And I suppose somebody had better have mine,"
Sprout mumbled gloomily. He could see the rain
washing out his chances of the yellow dinghy; for a
moment, even brownies didn't seem to matter.

"Anyway, somebody can have Tilly's," he added as
a more sensible afterthought.

"That still makes one missing," said Eileen. "Besides, why should poor little Tilly suffer?"

Just as she said it, there was a great howl from the
lounge; an unmistakable Tilly-howl.

Eileen put her head around the lounge door and was
trying to tell Tilly, above the din, that she could have a
brownie after all, when Sprout's mother said:

"It's not that. She's just swallowed the dice."

"She would!" said Sprout.

"Was it a big one?" Eileen asked.

"No," wailed Tilly, "but now we can't go on

playing. And I was winning!" she spluttered indignantly. "I just went up a big ladder, and Mommy said it said 'Have Another Go,' and —"

"You shouldn't put dice in your mouth," said Sprout. It was typical of Tilly that even playing Chutes and Ladders, she had to go and have an accident.

"I want another dice!"

"Well, we haven't got one," her mother sighed.

"I want to go and buy one!"

"We can't; it's raining. It's too wet to go out."

At the word "out," Chops looked up hopefully. And then Sprout had a good idea.

"I'll go!" he said. "I'll go and buy her new dice!"

"But Sprout, dear —"

"I've got my raincoat and my boots, and Raymond's got that silly plastic hat. I can borrow that, and anyway Chops ought to go for a walk!"

Sprout figured that if only they would let him out, he could cover a lot more shops before lunchtime. And he knew that his mother would be glad of anything to console Tilly, and that Eileen might like to have Chops out of the way.

He was quite right. His mother was a little doubtful at first, but Eileen said, "A little rain never did anybody any harm; otherwise, they'd all be dead in Ireland long ago!"

So off Sprout went.

Raymond, of course, stayed in because of his cold.

Sprout did feel slightly guilty when his mother said what a good, kind boy he was to go out by himself in the rain, just for Tilly.

But he forgot both the guilt and the rain in his excitement over finding two more things for his list even before he arrived at the toy shop where they sold dice: a tiny doll's boot among some licorice sticks in the candy store, and a rubberband around a doughnut in the bakery.

Then Chops stopped at the butcher's and wouldn't budge.

"Don't be silly," Sprout told him. "They haven't got a red spot on their window. That store's no good."

But Chops thought it was much the best store of all. Sprout tugged and pulled until the chain bit into his hand, but Chops obstinately stood there sniffing bones and sausages.

"Having trouble?" asked a voice behind him. It was Commander Piper, wearing a spotless navy blue raincoat and a yellow rain hat. Sprout knew that the Commander took his daily walk whatever the weather. Mrs. Lupin said you could see he had been in the Navy; he always looked smart, rain or shine.

But before Sprout had time to gasp "Hello," Chops had said it in his own special way.

In a matter of seconds, the Commander was covered with mud from head to foot.

"Down, Chops!" Sprout yelled. "I'm sorry," he said, "he's just glad to see you."

The Commander looked at his raincoat, looked at Sprout, glared at Chops, turned on his heel, and marched away.

"You shouldn't have done that," Sprout told Chops.

But Chops only wagged his woolly tail. Sprout did at least manage to heave him away from the butcher's to a stop outside the men's clothing store, which was the next shop with a red spot.

Sprout stared at the dummy figures of a boy and a man. Both had yellowish hands and faces, gray eyes, and smiles showing tiny white teeth. He stared at them up and down and on each side; he stared at the vests, pajamas, and pullovers pinned to the windows around them; he stared at the dummies' pointed feet and their chipped fingers. As for what was "wrong"—well, as far as he could see, everything in that window was wrong.

Suddenly there was a loud, high wail. Even higher and louder than Tilly's howl. A siren. And Sprout knew what it meant, because the ice-cream man had told him. It went off every day at the Seabay plastics factory, to announce the lunch break.

"Jiminy," Sprout said to Chops, "lunchtime!"

Chops was immediately all attention and eager to go wherever Sprout suggested. What was more, Sprout had seen a distant blue break in the sky. There was hope for the afternoon. And he certainly didn't want to miss his lunch.

"You poor boy, did you have to go far?" his mother asked. "Better get those wet things off."

"Is it big? Is it black and white?" Tilly demanded.

"Is what?"

"The dice!"

"Oh," said Sprout. "I forgot."

"But Sprout!" his mother exclaimed. "That's what you *went* for!"

Sprout said nothing. There really wasn't anything to say. Tilly started to make a fuss, so her mother hustled her into the dining room.

"Come on, let's think what you can be for the Costume Competition tomorrow. Goodness, we don't have much time if we have to make something!"

Sprout grunted. *"We've* only got till tonight," he muttered to Raymond.

"How many this morning?"

"Two. That makes six."

"Four more to get. We'll never do it," Raymond said, sneezing into his chicken pot pie.

Again, Sprout felt more determined than ever.

"The Commander's late," said Eileen when she cleared away the plates. "Funny. It's not like him."

At that moment the Commander strode in, looking pink and peeved.

"Sorry," he snapped. "Had to change course. Drugstore. Cleaning stuff." He sat down and glared at Sprout. There was a strong smell of cleaning fluid.

"Must have had tar on his paws." The Commander transferred the glare to Chops, who blinked back with complete goodwill.

"You were lucky to find the drugstore open," said Eileen cheerfully. "They close for lunch. I know, because once I was desperate for a corn plaster, and —"

"No more potato," said the Commander hastily. He had no wish to discuss Eileen's corns over his chicken pot pie. "Brussels sprouts. Frozen, I suppose. Like the one I saw in the drugstore window."

Sprout froze to attention.

"Don't know what they're coming to, these stores nowadays. I told the druggist: 'You ought to be reported to the Health Department. Brussels sprouts behind the aspirin—what next?' I said. He actually had the nerve to tell me it was only a small one!"

Sprout tried not to smile. Raymond looked at him and spread out seven fingers on the table.

"It's clearing up," said Sprout. "We can all go out this afternoon." He could see that even Raymond had brightened at this free gift of another thing for the list.

Certainly the afternoon promised well. The bit of blue that Sprout had seen in the sky widened to a great expanse; leaves glittered; Eileen hung out a line of dish towels; and there were butterflies on the daisies.

Sprout could hardly wait to be off. In fact, he didn't wait; he and Raymond shot out while Tilly was still looking for her spade.

"See you on the beach!"

The three stores they hadn't covered were the men's clothing store, the toy shop, and Tubby Trotter's Sports Store, which also had a red spot.

"Let's start with that," said Sprout. "Then you can see the dinghy."

"But we pass the men's store on the way," Raymond pointed out.

"I hate that store."

"Still, we've got to do it."

"Oh, all right. Maybe you'll see more than I did."

And, in fact, Raymond did. Looking narrowly at the smiling dummies of the boy and the man, he hissed: "His teeth!"

"What about them?" asked Sprout. "They're too small. Never saw a man with teeth like—"

"The third one on the right. Top teeth. There's something on it!"

Sprout peered hard.

"Hey, it looks like a stamp!"

"It is a stamp. I can see the jagged edge."

"Well, good. We'll write it down when we get back. Now let's go and look at the dinghy."

So they went and stared in the window of Trotter's Sports Store. Raymond agreed that it really was a good dinghy, almost as good as the canoes in Burma.

"Forget Burma," said Sprout. "What's *wrong*?"

But stare as they would, they couldn't see anything at all wrong in Tubby's window.

"We'd better go to the beach," warned Raymond, "or they'll be wondering."

Reluctantly Sprout went, with Chops pulling him along.

But as soon as they met his family, he said:

"All right, I'll go and get Tilly's dice now." That would take care of the toy shop, anyway.

But then Tilly had to go and say, "I don't want dice anymore. I don't like that game."

"But you were playing it all this morning!" protested Sprout.

"Well, what *do* you want?"

"I want to be a shrimp," said Tilly.

"What d'you mean? Don't be stupid!"

"In the Costume Competition," sighed his mother. "She's taken it into her head to go as a shrimp. Goodness knows how we're going to manage it."

"She's too fat," said Sprout.

"Well, what about you?" Tilly retorted. "You're as fat as . . ." Words failed her.

"But I don't want to be a shrimp," said Sprout crossly. "I'm going to get an ice-cream cone." And he stumped up toward the boardwalk.

Sprout did want an ice-cream cone, of course, but he also wanted to consult somebody sensible. Raymond didn't seem to be of much use, and Ted the ice-cream man was one of Sprout's best friends in Seabay, partly because Sprout was one of Ted's best customers.

"So you're in on that game, are you?" said Ted when Sprout had explained. "Well, good luck to you, young man, that's all I can say." He handed Sprout a cone; chocolate this time.

"D'you think many people get them all right?"

"Search me."

"D'you think many go in for it?"

"Thousands, I imagine. Well, look at the place! Look at it!" He waved his hand toward the boardwalk and the beach, crowded with people enjoying themselves more energetically than ever, after the morning's rain.

"My dad used to tell me stories about Seabay —

when it was a couple of blankets and an ice-cream truck on Saturdays."

"What, not even cotton candy?"

"Cotton candy!" said Ted. "You must be joking! Half dead, the place was, thirty years ago. Regatta? They wouldn't have been able to spell it out, let alone have one. Ah, you can't say Seabay hasn't moved with the times. Look at that, for a start."

He pointed upward and waved.

A yellow helicopter was flying over the bay. It came down quite low, and Sprout could see the pilot in the open-sided cockpit.

Of course, Sprout had seen helicopters before, but never so close that you could notice the pilot's face.

This pilot, apparently lying on his side at a great open window, came near enough to give Ted a grin and a wave; then he was away.

The machine looked as bright as a dandelion, as busy as some inquisitive foreign insect, over the slate-blue sea.

"Hey! Didn't he come near!" Sprout gasped admiringly.

"That was young Reg," said Ted. "He's at the RAF station, on the other side of the bluff. His kids come for cones, most days. With regards to which, was you thinking along the lines of another one?" The chocolate one had disappeared.

"I'd better not," said Sprout. "I've spent nearly all my money. Besides, I've got to cover these shops."

"Old Tubby Trotter will have made *his* hard," said Ted, "to make up for having his turn giving a prize. All the shopkeepers take turns, see, year to year. I bet old Tubby looked down in the mouth when they told him it was his turn."

"Why?"

"Oh, you don't know Tubby! It'd hurt him to give away a Ping-Pong ball, let alone a dinghy. So he'll make the clue as hard as he can, in hopes nobody gets it."

Sprout closed his mouth very tight and marched away. He decided to concentrate entirely on Tubby Trotter's.

He got Raymond to go with him, and they both glued their noses to the pane. There was a long silence.

"I don't believe there *is* anything wrong," muttered Raymond.

"There must be." Sprout's gaze kept coming back to the yellow dinghy—so near and yet so far.

"He might have cheated," Raymond said.

"He couldn't. People'd find out."

"Well, there's nothing wrong in there. If there was, *I* should have found it." Raymond looked rather sulky.

"Go round it all again."

"I have. Oh come on, it's no good. We'll be here all day."

"I don't care if I am."

"What, and miss tea?"
Sprout tightened his mouth.
"*And* dinner?"
Sprout frowned.
"It's hamburgers for dinner," he said. "Eileen told me. With french fries!"
He stared gloomily at Tubby Trotter's all-too-tidy

window. A place for everything and everything in its place: Ping-Pong balls in boxes; badminton birdies stacked neatly on top of each other, feathers downward; baseball bats and tennis rackets crisscrossed at perfect right angles; a row of footballs strung up at the back alternately—rugby, soccer, rugby, soccer, with a boxing glove at each end. Sprout had to agree that they might stand there all day without seeing anything wrong.

"I know!" he said. "Let's go and see if it's tea time and, if it is, bring some cookies back here. We might feel better. Maybe we just need food."

"There's still the toy shop."

"Oh, that'll probably be easy as pie. Come on."

Sprout made his way purposefully cookie-wards. Mrs. Lupin always packed tea for the beach. Sprout honestly felt that a cookie and a few sandwiches, with perhaps a piece of cake, might sharpen his wits.

Tilly greeted them with a broad smile and a new shrimping-net. It seemed that she had pestered her father into taking her to the toy shop to buy one.

"Because if I'm going to *be* a shrimp, we want to see what one looks like. They're not a very nice color."

"Have you had tea?"

"No. This net was the last one. And guess what it was tied on to the door with!"

"Let's have tea now," said Sprout.

"It wasn't string and it wasn't rope. Guess what it was?"

"Who cares?" said Sprout.

But Raymond suddenly looked sharp and narrowed his eyes.

"Well, what?" he asked Tilly.

"Ha, ha!" she said, delighted to be properly noticed. "You'd never guess! So I'll tell you. It was a shoelace."

"I don't see anything so funny in that," said Raymond.

"A licorice shoelace!" Tilly announced with triumph. "And they don't even sell licorice. The saleslady told me not to tell."

Sprout and Raymond looked at each other.

"But you *are* telling," said Sprout. However pleased he felt, he still thought Tilly should be put in her place.

"Oh, it doesn't matter telling *you*," she said airily. "She meant *people*!"

Sprout didn't bother to answer this. Raymond was whispering in his ear, anyway.

"It must be It! Now there's only one more!"

"We've got till eight o'clock," said Sprout, and stuffed in a honey sandwich. This, and Tilly's bit of news, made him feel much more comfortable. By the fourth sandwich and second cookie, he didn't see how they could fail.

He was prepared, if necessary, to go and challenge Tubby Trotter in person and ask him face to face whether it was really true that there was something wrong in his window. Sprout figured that you could generally tell, face to face, if a person was lying.

After tea, he and Raymond went back to the sports store. But still no luck. Raymond was rather cross; Sprout was furious. He remembered what Ted had said about Tubby's making it difficult, but this was ridiculous. Altogether, they must have looked in that wretched sports window for nearly two hours.

"We'll have to come back after supper, that's all," said Sprout.

"What's the use? It'll be just the same. Besides, we've never been out by ourselves after supper."

"Chops'll be glad," said Sprout.

"I don't see any point in it," mumbled Raymond gloomily.

"Tubby Trotter will," said Sprout.

"What d'you mean?"

"If we don't find the thing, I'll bang on his door and make him come out and explain."

"You can't do that!"

"Wait and see," Sprout said.

3

At a quarter past seven, armed with their list, and with Chops being very good on his chain, they stood once more outside that last window.

At twenty past, to Raymond's great alarm, Sprout banged on the door at the side of the shop.

"What are you going to say?" whispered Raymond anxiously.

Sprout just tightened his mouth. After a few moments he banged again, more loudly.

Footsteps. Chops began to wag his short tail. He was very much surprised at this evening outing and hoped it might lead to some excitement. Even an extra dinner.

Tubby Trotter didn't look like the sort of person who would give an extra dinner to anybody, let alone a dog.

The "Tubby" must have been a sour joke; he was, in fact, one of the thinnest people Sprout had ever seen. Even his hair was thin. He had hollow cheeks and a stringy neck and spectacles with very thin steel rims.

"Well?" he demanded.

Sprout explained about the window.

"We thought you might have made a mistake," he said.

"Mistake? I don't make mistakes," snapped Tubby. "Now go away."

He was just going to shut the door, but Chops had pushed his big face inside because he thought he smelled gravy.

"Are you *sure*?" asked Sprout. He looked at Tubby very hard.

"What d'you mean, sure? And get that dog's nose out.".

"All right," said Sprout, "I will, if you go and look in the window yourself."

"And why should I look in my own window?"

Sprout glared and gave Chop's tail a slight shove farther into the doorway.

"Because we think you're cheating," he said. "And if you are, we shall *tell*!"

"How dare you!" gasped Tubby Trotter. "Go away at once, you terrible little boys! Be off, the pair of you!"

"No," said Sprout. Anyone who called him a "little boy" was asking for trouble.

"You look in that window," he insisted, "and you swear, cross your heart, that it's not a cheat."

Instantly, though only for a second, he saw that look of lying cross Tubby's face. He could also see that Tubby was not a dog-lover. Sprout always said, afterward, that it was Chops who saved the day.

For, upon a promise that Chops would be removed at once, Tubby agreed to go and look in his window. The odd thing was that, instead of looking in it from the outside, like an ordinary person, Tubby dived into the shop and appeared *inside* the window.

Sprout watched him closely. Tubby fiddled with the footballs hanging on a string at the back and then with the boxing gloves. Very quickly, he dived out of the window again and reappeared at the shop door.

But Sprout's eyes were quick, too. And his face glowed pink with triumph and indignation.

"That banana!" he said. "It wasn't there before! You just put it there!"

"I don't know what you're talking about," muttered Tubby. He darted into the entrance to his own stairs and slammed the door in their faces. Chops nearly got his whiskers caught in the door.

"What banana?" asked Raymond. He had been too nervous to look or think clearly.

"In that boxing glove," said Sprout. "Sticking out."

Raymond gaped. Certainly there was about half an inch of banana showing in the left-hand glove.

"It couldn't have been there before," he began.

"Of course it couldn't," said Sprout. "Anyway, quick, put it down. Where's the paper? What's the time?"

It was ten to eight. Chops was amazed and delighted suddenly to be allowed to run almost as fast as he could. In fact, once he was set in the right direction, he tore along so that Sprout, on the other end of the chain, hardly touched the ground. They arrived at the Regatta Office at two minutes to the hour and handed in the paper.

Sprout took a deep breath.

"And I bet," he said, "we're the only ones who've got it. Because that banana was *new*!"

"It might have fallen down inside the glove," said Raymond fairly, "and he might not have known."

Sprout said nothing.

They decided to give Chops the reward of a last run on the beach. The tide was out, so they threw stones for him. In the evening, the beach was empty except for a few booted figures who stood far off near the edge of the water, doing mysterious things with pails and garden spades. Ted the ice-cream man had told Sprout that they were getting lugworms for bait. Sprout thought this was a dull thing to do, and Chops, having made a blundering, woolly bounce at one of the pails, decided that running after stones was better. He was really quite sensitive about being yelled at.

So they all three had a happy half hour and arrived back at Mrs. Lupin's to find Sprout's mother only just beginning to worry. She had almost forgotten the time, in the fluster of trying to work out Tilly's shrimp costume.

Wednesday was going to be a busy day. Mrs. Chad and Albina were arriving right after lunch, and the Costume Competition started at half past two. But far more important to Sprout was the fact that the Win-a-Dinghy results were to be given out "some time during the afternoon."

He went to bed in a state of tense impatience. He lay rigid for a long time, thinking of the yellow dinghy. From his bed, he could see a square of dark blue sky through the open window. There were stars; it might be a fine day tomorrow. Suddenly a new star appeared. No, not a star. It was red, and moving. An airplane. But then it dropped out of sight below the windowsill. A helicopter, then. Maybe the one he had seen in the afternoon, flown by Ted's friend, young Reg. The afternoon seemed a long time ago; and tomorrow afternoon still longer ahead. The little red light rose again, soared diagonally across the window, and disappeared.

Sprout went to sleep.

On Wednesday morning, the sun was shining.

"Good. It's going to be nice for the Chads," said Sprout's mother. She was frantically cutting up pieces of shrimp-pink paper. Sprout's father had the job of chopping the ends off two large black-headed knitting needles, for eyes.

"I imagine Albina will want to come and see the Competition," said Sprout's mother. "But if she doesn't, you must play with her nicely."

Sprout said nothing.

"She may prefer to go swimming; after all, she's only got one afternoon. Or you could take her on the boardwalk."

The morning seemed endless. Tilly did nothing but chatter about shrimps, until Sprout got so fed up that he told her she didn't stand a chance. Shrimps weren't that color, anyway.

"I'm a *cooked* one!" squeaked Tilly with tears in her eyes; and their mother asked Sprout why he was being so unkind.

"You could have had a costume yourself if you'd wanted to," she said, "only you didn't seem interested."

"I'm not," said Sprout.

He wasn't even really interested in lunch and actually refused a third strawberry tart.

"When does afternoon begin?" he muttered to Raymond.

"After noon, of course. Noon's at twelve."

"Then it's now! They might be giving out the results now! And if we're not there . . ."

"Their bus doesn't arrive until two," called his mother, but Sprout had gone. "Well, it's nice of him to be so anxious to go and meet them," she said with some surprise. "Mrs. Chad'll appreciate that."

Of course, Sprout didn't go near the bus stop, but they did all meet on the beach. Albina spotted Sprout first.

"Look, there he is! The fat one with the cotton candy!"

"Now then, my girl, don't you be rude," her mother told her. "Be a good thing if *you* could get a bit more flesh on you. And look out for those white sandals, there might be tar."

The two figures—Mrs. Chad's like a huge flowered armchair and Albina's like a pin—made their way across the pebbles to where Sprout was sitting. Sprout was gazing up at the bandstand on the boardwalk. It had loudspeakers fitted to its roof; at any moment he expected to hear them bellow out the Great Announcement. He could hardly bear to say so much as "Hello" to the Chads.

"What's she all done up in paper for?" Albina pointed to Tilly, who stood with whiskers of pink crepe paper fluttering, while her mother made last-minute adjustments to the costume. One of these was to tie the paper together below her knees, so that she looked as if she had a tail.

"Bless her, she's a herring!" said Mrs. Chad. She had already heard the loudspeakers advertising the Costume Competition.

"Shrimp!" said Tilly indignantly, her black knitting-needle-head eyes waggling on her pink woolly hat.

"Attention, everybody!" A huge voice commanded the beach. Sprout stopped eating his cotton candy. "Will all entrants for the Costume Competition please assemble NOW on the boardwalk."

Sprout went on eating.

"Oh dear," said Tilly's mother, "come on, we must hurry."

She was trying to tie Tilly's knees together with pink tape.

"She'll never be able to walk like that," observed Albina. Tilly at once tried to take a step and fell flat on her face. She started to wail.

"Never mind, upsy-daisy," said Mrs. Chad, and put her back on her feet. "Dear little shrimp!" she beamed. "I could just eat one like you for my tea!" And she picked Tilly up and started to carry her toward the boardwalk.

"I *told* you she couldn't walk," said Albina again.

"No shrimps can," grunted Sprout. He wished they would all be quiet, or go away, in case the Voice said something really important.

"How's she going to get around in the Grand Parade, then?" Albina persisted. She had seen many Costume Competitions before.

"One of us ought to have gone as a shrimping-net," suggested Raymond. Sprout gave him a scornful look; how could he make jokes, at a time like this?

"Attention everybody," said the Voice again. But it was only another announcement about the Costume Competition.

"You're crumpling all her whiskers!" Albina called out to Mrs. Chad, who was still staggering up the beach with Tilly.

"Why don't you come and help, then, instead of standing there!"

Tilly's mother followed after them with an emergency roll of pink crepe paper.

"If there's carrying to be done, I'd better come," said Tilly's father. He knew that Tilly was a hefty weight, even for Mrs. Chad.

"Are you comin' to watch it, then?" yelled Mrs. Chad over her shoulder at Albina.

Albina shook her head.

"What?" shrieked Mrs. Chad.

"I want to swim!" piped Albina. "My bikini!" she wailed, and suddenly rushed after her mother. She dived into Mrs. Chad's handbag and came back to where Sprout and Raymond were sitting. Two tiny pink frilled objects dangled from her arm.

"They say it's all right," she said, "as long as you

come in with me. You'll have to look the other way while I put these on, though."

"I'm not swimming," said Sprout. The idea of being in the water when the Great Announcement was made!

Albina was struggling to get on the pink bikini under her yellow cotton dress.

"You've *got* to come," she said, "or I can't. And I'm only down for the day!" Her black eyes looked accusingly at Sprout over a bundle of yellow.

"*He'll* go in." Sprout indicated Raymond. "Besides, he can swim." It was the first time he had ever openly admitted he couldn't swim.

"All right, then, wait while I do my hair."

Expertly she screwed her hair up into a knob on top and fastened it with a purple plastic butterfly. Sprout wished they would both get into the water and leave him alone to listen.

And so they did. Raymond went first, with a great deal of splashing and then a duck-dive; Albina with squeaks, jumps, shivers, giggles, chatterings of teeth, and hunchings of sharp shoulder blades.

"Ladies and gentlemen!" said the Voice. "I have an important announcement to make! Attention please!"

Sprout forgot Raymond and Albina completely.

"We have just received the final results of the Win-a-Dinghy Competition!"

Sprout got goose bumps all over.

"This competition," the Voice boomed on, "was for "spot-what's-wrong-in-the-shop." Ten shops in Seabay took part. Eight hundred and forty-seven entries were received."

Sprout froze. Eight hundred and forty-seven!

"—And, believe it or not, out of those, more than seven hundred spotted nine out of the ten things correctly! You clever people! How about a little cheer for seven hundred pairs of sharp eyes?"

Over the loudspeakers came a crackling, shrill, broken kind of squeak from the Seabay Girls' Band, who wore white satin uniforms and had been placed around the bandstand in order to back up the announcer.

Sprout clutched Chops's tail and sat riveted to the sand.

"But what about the winner?" The Voice paused dramatically. "The lucky winner of this fabulous dinghy! Here it is: I'm going to ask our generous old friend Tubby Trotter to hold it up now! Are you there, Tubby?"

There was some more crackling over the loudspeakers. Tubby Trotter appeared on the bandstand and held the yellow dinghy upright. The Seabay Girls' Band gave a dutiful round of applause.

Sprout was on the point of exploding. Why didn't they get on with it? Chops looked patiently around, wondering why his tail was being held so hard.

"Very well, then," boomed the announcer, "here is

the news I know you've all been waiting for! The winner of the shop-spotting prize dinghy, the one person to get ten out of ten correct answers, and who in a moment I shall ask to come up and receive the fabulous prize from the hands of Tubby Trotter himself . . . the name is . . . (give us the paper, Mavis) . . ."

These last words were muttered with a crackle that nearly made Sprout's hair stand straight up on end.

". . . Thank you, dear. Well, the name of the lucky winner is: *Mr. Rupert E. Smith*! I'll repeat that. Mr. Rupert E. Smith. So, ladies and gentlemen, if Mr. Rupert E. Smith is here, will he please come up and claim this magnificent prize? Now, I realize that it

may take him some moments to make his way through this happy crowd, so meanwhile, I have just received the names of the lucky winners of the Costume Competition . . ."

Sprout heard no more. It always took him a few moments to remember that his real name was Rupert. The "Smith" he never bothered with, and the "E" was a thing he would much rather have forgotten — but he had put it in defiantly after seeing that banana in Tubby Trotter's window.

"Rupert E. Smith," he had signed himself.

And now!

Chops was surprised to find his tail so suddenly free.

Sprout staggered up the sand. He didn't even look back to yell at Raymond, who was somewhere in the water with Albina. Sprout didn't care where he was.

Chops padded after him and they arrived at the top of the bandstand steps together.

"I'm Rupert E. Smith," said Sprout.

The announcer's face broke into a big delighted grin. Tubby Trotter's mouth fell open—and for a moment he looked anything but pleased—but then he had to pull himself together and make the presentation. Sprout was too full of pride, amazement, and joy to notice what the announcer was saying or how nervously Tubby was glancing at Chops. His mind was entirely upon the dinghy. In a daze, he heard some clapping and saw a microphone being held in front of his mouth.

"Come on," said the announcer, "what did you say the 'E' stood for?"

"What 'E'?" asked Sprout.

Titters from the Girls' Band.

"Between Rupert and Smith," said the announcer. "Let's have a guess, then. What about 'Ercules?"

General giggles. All Sprout wanted to do was to get the precious dinghy down those steps and into the water.

"Entwhistle," he muttered.

Roars of laughter. Sprout got pink all over; but then he clutched the dinghy and felt that it was worth it—worth almost anything—to call such a glorious thing his own.

He hardly noticed at all when people laughed to see him struggle down the steps with it.

Raymond was just wading out of the water with Albina, who was pale blue all over.

"Look what I've got! Look!" yelled Sprout.

"Hey! D'you mean we won it?" Raymond streaked over the pebbles; he had tough feet.

"Well, a bit more me than you," said Sprout. After all, it had been his idea; it was his name on the paper; and he was the one who had had to say "Entwhistle."

Albina stood wobbling on the stones a few inches away from the edge of the water.

"I'm cold," she said, clutching herself with blue arms and wobbling more than ever.

"Well, come and get dressed!" shouted Sprout. He himself was as warm as toast and much too excited to bother about Albina.

"I can't!" she wailed. "I want my sandals!"

Neither Sprout nor Raymond heard this; they were both gloating over the dinghy.

"Come on," said Sprout to Raymond.

He began to drag the dinghy to the edge of the water.

"SPROUT!" It was his mother's voice; and in the background, a terribly familiar wailing, much more high-pitched than Albina's.

Tilly.

Her father was carrying her, Mrs. Chad waddled behind, and Sprout's mother hurried forward anxiously.

"Sprout, what are you doing?" she asked. "What's that thing? Where's Albina? Good gracious, she looks frozen!"

Whereupon Mrs. Chad rushed down the beach and gathered up Albina, whose sodden top-knot dripped all down her Mom's best dress.

And Tilly howled.

"Look what I've won," said Sprout.

Nobody really looked; at least, not properly and admiringly, as Sprout had expected.

"Oh, pipe down!" his father said to Tilly.

"Look at her! She's blue! She'll catch her death!" gasped Mrs. Chad. She dumped the shivering Albina on Sprout's beach towel.

"I want a prize! Why didn't I get a prize?" wailed Tilly. "It's not fair!"

Her father put her down beside Albina. Her shrimp costume was torn to ribbons and damp with tears.

"She had to wait up there for half an hour," said Sprout's mother. "We tied her legs up, ready, but —"

"This is my dinghy," said Sprout. He couldn't understand why they took so little notice. His father was mopping his brow and muttering about being a beast of burden, his mother was trying to comfort Tilly, and Mrs. Chad was helping Albina back into the yellow dress.

"There, now; feel a bit warmer, dear?"

"No," said Albina. Her teeth were chattering and her face and arms and legs looked a terrible purple against the yellow.

"Sprout, why didn't you look after her?" scolded his mother. "You ought to have known better!"

Sprout said nothing. Tilly kept sniffing and spluttering about its not being fair, and Albina shivered more violently than ever.

"She'd better go and sit in the car," said Sprout's mother, "out of the wind."

"You *won* that?" His father had just become aware of the dinghy.

"Yes. It's free!" Sprout beamed.

"Ones like it cost forty-five dollars in the shop," said Raymond.

"Where's the car key gone?" Sprout's mother asked. "I just put it down here a minute ago." She was groveling around in the sand.

"That dog's buried it, I bet," said Mrs. Chad. Neither she nor Albina had ever been fond of Chops. Albina shuddered and gave him a baleful glare.

"Well, we've got to find it," Sprout's mother said.

"Anyway, goodbye," said Sprout.

"What d'you mean, 'goodbye'?"

"Well, we're taking this into the water."

"Oh no you're not; not until we've found the car key. You just come and help look."

Albina sneezed. "Oh dear," moaned Mrs. Chad, "she'll be getting the flu next!"

"Silly place to put a car key down," muttered Sprout's father. "Come on, everybody help."

Sprout realized that the sooner they found the silly key, the sooner he would be able to take the dinghy out. So he scrabbled with the others. Only Tilly sat doing nothing.

"Why don't you help?" Sprout grunted at her furiously.

"I can't. I'm a shrimp."

Sprout was too impatient for words.

Albina sneezed again.

"Look," said Sprout's father, "I did leave the trunk of the car unlocked. Maybe she could jump in there just for the time being?"

"Here, wrap this blanket around you and go sit there until we've found the key," said Sprout's mother. "You go with her, Sprout."

"Why?"

"To show her the car, of course."

"She can find it," said Sprout. "It's red." He couldn't bear the idea of going a step farther than necessary away from his dinghy.

"I'll come with you, dear," said Mrs. Chad.

"Baby!" muttered Sprout.

"I'm not a baby!" piped Albina; she had sharp ears. "I'll go by myself, so there!"

And she trailed up the beach, swathed in the blanket that they generally sat on.

"It's all sandy, with no blanket," said Tilly. She got up and began to wander around, filling her plastic bucket with pebbles. Her shrimp whiskers streamed in the wind.

"Haven't we got a spare key?" Sprout asked. He was extremely fed up with this waste of time.

"No," said his father crossly. "I left it at home."

Suddenly Tilly said, "Look!"

There on the top of her bucket lay the key.

"It was in the sand where Chops was sitting," she said. "*Good* Chops!"

"I don't see much good about that," said Mrs. Chad. "All this trouble."

"Here, you boys, go and open the car for Albina," said Sprout's father.

"*Us?*" Sprout was highly indignant. "But . . ."

"Go on, make yourselves useful for once. After all, Tilly found the key — and she hasn't even won a prize."

There were times when Sprout recognized a brisk firmness in his father's voice which allowed no argument. This was one of those times.

He and Raymond hurried up to the parking lot.

"Here you are, you can come out, we've got the key!" shouted Sprout. He quickly unlocked the passenger door. Raymond was standing by the half-open trunk.

"She's not here," he said.

"She must be."

"She's not. Look."

Sprout looked. Certainly the trunk contained neither blanket nor Albina.

"Hi! What's up? Lost something?"

It was Ted, pushing one of his small ice-cream wagons a little nearer to the dune.

"Yes. A girl," said Sprout.

"What, a scrawny little thing with a blanket around her?"

"Yes."

"Well, she got into the trunk of a car a few minutes ago. Couldn't help noticing. I thought 'Poor little mite, she looks cold. No good offering *her* ice cream,' I thought. 'Hot soup'd be more the idea.'"

"But she's not *in* the trunk," said Sprout.

"Wasn't that car," said Ted. "Darker red than that; parked just . . . oh. It's gone."

He indicated an empty parking space.

Sprout and Raymond stared at each other.

"That silly girl!" Sprout burst out. "She's gotten into the *wrong car!*"

4

To say that what happened next was a fuss would be to put it mildly.

Sprout hated fusses at the best of times; but suddenly here he was, surrounded by his parents being horrified, Mrs. Chad being distraught, Ted trying to describe the dark red car, and Raymond saying things like "They might be halfway to London by now. Or even Manchester."

"Must call the police. Nine-nine-nine," said Sprout's father.

"Nearest phone booth, just up there, sir," said Ted. Sprout's father rushed off.

"She might be smothered!" wailed Mrs. Chad. "Did they shut the trunk? Did they bang it shut?"

"Couldn't say," said Ted. "Well, I never even saw them go, did I? Noticed her get in, that's all. Been such a run on pops ever since . . ."

Mrs. Chad burst into tears. Sprout's mother turned on him.

"You see?" she said desperately. "I told you!"

"What?"

"You should have come up with her, shown her the car!"

"If anything's happened to her . . . oh dear, the poor little thing! I should never have gone to that Costume Competition. How *could* I? Take somebody else's child, and leave my own to . . . oh, I can't bear to think of it!" Mrs. Chad wailed, collapsing in a wet bundle on the low stone wall around the geraniums.

"Cheer up, I imagine she'll be all right," said Ted. "Here, have an ice cream cone. On me. Any color you like!" He got ready with his scoop, but Mrs. Chad was past thinking of ice cream. And Sprout knew better than to take up the offer for himself, though he did think "what a waste."

"By the way, where *is* Tilly?" his mother asked

sharply. They had all rushed up from the beach in such a panic. . . .

"And where's my *dinghy*?" shouted Sprout.

He stood aghast.

There was the place on the beach where they always sat.

There was Tilly's red plastic bucket.

There were the bath towels, green and orange, and the big picnic basket.

But no yellow dinghy.

"It's gone!" said Sprout.

"I can't see her anywhere!" said his mother. "Now where on earth . . .?"

Sprout was already on the beach. He dashed down to the edge of the water, where Chops stood barking.

"Chops! Come here! Where is it? Who stole it?"

His mother came panting up behind him.

"Have you seen her?"

"It *can't* have gone!" Sprout stared at the empty space on the sand; he couldn't believe his eyes.

"Her bucket and spade are still here — surely she can't have gone far. . . ." said Sprout's mother, scanning the beach. Chops went on barking; Sprout was almost beside himself.

"Oh, SHUT UP!" he yelled at Chops.

Whereupon Chops did a very unusual thing. Simply sat down facing the water and howled.

And then Sprout saw—far out beyond all the

swimmers, beyond all the other dinghies—a small pink figure bobbing on something yellow. It appeared to be waving, but it also appeared to be getting smaller and farther away every moment. The tide was going out, and the stiff breeze was off the land.

"It's Tilly!" shrieked Sprout. "She's gone and *taken* it! Before I'd even had a ride!"

His mother went deathly pale.

"She's drifting away!" she gasped. "Help! Somebody go after her! She's going out to sea!"

Several people nearby on the beach looked around, saw what had happened, and ran to the edge of the water in dismay.

"Too far to swim," said one.

"There's a strong current out there," said another.

"I'll get Dad," shouted Sprout, tearing back to the boardwalk.

His father had just come back from the phone booth, and was trying to console Mrs. Chad.

"Now don't worry, the police are alerting all their patrol cars. She can't have gotten far yet. . . ." he was saying.

"Tilly's gotten far!" panted Sprout, pointing out to sea.

His father went into action like a rocket.

"Nine-nine-nine again, and ask for Helicopter Emergency," Ted shouted after him as he dashed back to the phone booth.

"She went and took it," Sprout said to Raymond. "My dinghy!"

"Oh my goodness gracious, what if she was to fall out?" said Mrs. Chad.

"She's heading for France," said Raymond.

"Oh, don't, don't!" Sprout's mother groaned. "You know how easily she falls out of things — oh, I can't bear it!"

"Hold on, Missus, soon as they get to young Reg, he'll be out there in a matter of minutes. If not seconds. They're very fast on the job, those boys," Ted said.

"What, the helicopter?" said Sprout.

"Oh dear, she's farther away than ever! It must be the current — oh, I wish they'd hurry!"

Sprout's mother stood twisting her handkerchief into knots.

"What a day, what a day!" Mrs. Chad kept saying. "I wish we'd never come!"

"Look! There you are — what did I tell you?" Ted's face cracked into a big smile. "There he is! There he goes!"

He pointed delightedly to the yellow helicopter, which seemed to have appeared from nowhere and was now whirring straight out over the sea.

"Even quicker'n you could get back from the phone booth," he nodded to Sprout's father, who had just run up with his hand shading his anxious eyes against the brightness of sea and sky.

"They certainly didn't lose much time," he said.

"Wish they'd be as quick with Albina," said Mrs. Chad.

"But what will they do? How will they get her? A helicopter can't land on the water, can it?" Sprout's mother sounded desperate.

"Not *on* it, no," said Ted. "Besides, if they got too close, the airstream might overturn the dinghy."

"But then how can they . . .?"

"Let a man down, that's what they do," said Ted confidently. "On a string. Well, cable, to be exact. It'll look like a string from here, though. You watch. You'll see."

Everyone on the beach was watching.

"Up to forty yards, they can get." said Ted. "Up to forty yards without capsizing her. Reg told me that." He was obviously proud of his inside knowledge and full of faith in Reg.

"Look! There he is! There he goes!"

"Who, Reg?" said Sprout.

"Fat lot of use, the pilot jumping out!" said Ted. "No — that's one of the other two. Look! See him?"

"No," said Sprout. His eyes were beginning to water from so much staring. Mrs. Chad fondly imagined that he was crying and patted his tuft.

"Yes! I can see him now!" Sprout's father clutched his mother's arm.

"Is that really a man?" she asked. It looked like a tiny gray crumb on a thread.

"Probably old Nobby," nodded Ted. "He's been the winchman on Reg's crew most of this season. There he goes. Look! He's down! He's got her! I bet he's got her! Wait for it, now. . . ."

"But what will he do with her?" his mother cried in alarm.

"Fasten her on and tell them to heave up," said Ted. "Don't worry, Missus, he won't drop her. As long as she don't panic. They can be a bit of trouble when they panic."

"She'll probably just howl," said Sprout's father.

"What about my dinghy?" said Sprout.

No one ever heard him. There was a sudden wave of excitement over the beach as people saw, not one gray crumb, but two — the second a very small one, but distinct — rising into the air from the far-off sea. Still the helicopter hovered. The cable became shorter, shorter; the crumbs nearer, nearer to the yellow insect – until suddenly they seemed to merge with it and be swallowed up.

"They're in! They've got her!" shouted Ted in triumph. "What about ice-cream cones all around, eh?"

The helicopter was flying swiftly inland.

"What about my *dinghy*?"

"What about Albina?" moaned Mrs. Chad. "Talk about rubber boats, at a time like this!"

"Yes, I'm surprised at you, Sprout!" burst out his

mother, suddenly angry because she was so much relieved.

"Look here," his father said, "one of us had better go to the airport, or wherever they'll land her. If she's cold, I bet she'll howl the place down."

Ted eagerly told him the way to the helicopter base.

"I'll come," said Sprout's mother. "I've got to see she's all right. Now where's that big blanket? Oh dear — of course, Albina. . . ."

She realized she had said the wrong thing. Mrs. Chad immediately burst into floods of tears.

"Now look, mom," said Ted, "you wait here with me, eh? This is where they'll bring her back to, and I bet they won't be long now. Come on, cheer up; remember the good old British police!"

"I know," wept Mrs. Chad. "My husband's one."

"Well, then, there you are!" said the cheerful Ted, as if that solved everything.

"We must go," said Sprout's father.

"I'm coming too," said Sprout. "Raymond can stay here."

He was determined to find out what they had done with his dinghy. He certainly hadn't seen it pulled up on that cable. His mouth was set in a very straight line indeed.

When they arrived at the RAF station, they were directed to an outlying group of low white buildings, flat-roofed and with a small airfield beyond, then into a room that had a long counter with a lot of mugs on it, and some cans, and a huge electric kettle.

There were three men with mugs in their hands.

As soon as they turned around, there was no need to say any more.

"Tilly!" gasped her mother.

There she was, wrapped in an army blanket, drinking cocoa.

Her mother dived forward; her father took one stride and lifted her up, blanket, mug, and all.

"Look out for my cocoa!" Tilly squeaked. No howls, no tears; her face simply looked pink with satisfaction.

"I had a ride in an airplane," she said. "*And* a swing on a big rope."

Sprout could hardly believe that anyone could be so stupid.

"It wasn't an airplane, and where's my dinghy?"

No one answered him. His parents were busy talking to the three men. The tallest one turned out to be Reg. There was a shorter, ginger-haired one, whom he introduced as his navigator; and a stocky, dark one called Nobby, who turned out to be the winchman. It was he who had gone down on the cable and actually brought up Tilly.

It was no use, at the moment, Sprout's asking anybody anything. Tilly seemed to be the center of attention, and thoroughly enjoying it.

". . . And was I surprised to find I'd picked up a

shrimp!" said Nobby. "Fattest little shrimp that ever came my way, eh?"

Sprout could stand no more.

"*Where's my dinghy?*" he shouted.

Nobby stopped teasing Tilly and turned around.

"Oh, that was yours, was it, sonny? Well, I'm afraid you won't be seeing that again."

Sprout stared.

"Had to sink it, see? Strict instructions."

Sprout went on staring.

"Show you the razor I used, if you like," said Nobby amiably.

"Can't leave empty inflatable boats drifting around," Reg explained. "Some other crew might see them and think there's been an accident. Our job is saving *people*, you see, not rubber boats."

Sprout took a deep breath. His speechlessness broke.

"You've sunk my dinghy!" he shouted. "My yellow dinghy, that I won!"

"But Tilly's safe. . . ." his mother began.

"At least you didn't have to pay for it. . . ." his father started to mumble.

But Sprout was halfway out of that room. He was afraid he might be going to cry.

"And I never even had a *ride* in it!" He slammed the door.

5

All the way back in the car, he was too furious and miserable to speak.

It was no comfort to hear his parents at last beginning to scold Tilly for her naughtiness. Then, when they had finished that, they started going on about Albina. Poor Albina, they said. Poor Mrs. Chad. . . .

"Let's hurry," said Sprout's mother.

Sprout sat in the back of the car in a state of disgust and rage. It was all Albina's fault. If it hadn't been for her, he would never have let the dinghy out of his sight.

His only possible comfort in the world, at the moment, was Chops, who looked out of his woolly bangs inquiringly and knew there was something wrong. But he couldn't help; only lick.

The car turned around the corner and into the parking lot.

"Look! Look, I believe she's there!" exclaimed Sprout's mother. "Yes, I can see them — they're waving! Oh, what a relief!"

"The police must have done some pretty smart work," said Sprout's father.

"Albina was a silly girl," said Tilly smugly, "to get into the wrong trunk."

Sprout nearly exploded. But his father said sharply: "That makes *two* silly girls."

Sprout hoped that Tilly got the point. All the same, no words could bring back his sunk dinghy.

Mrs. Chad was radiant.

"They just brought her!" she said. "Three very nice officers — ooh and look there, you've got Tilly back, too! What a blessing!"

"I told you," beamed Ted. "I said it'd be all right, didn't I?"

Sprout nudged Raymond aside.

"It isn't all right at all," he said, and explained.

"What, *sunk* it?" said Raymond blankly.

"Now then, you boys," said Sprout's mother,

"we're all going to have tea. And high time, too. Poor Albina looks like she's starving."

"I'm all right," said Albina. "They gave me candy and things. When they found what they'd done. The people in the car."

"Ever so nice they were to her, and I should think so, too!" said Mrs. Chad.

"Jelly beans," said Albina.

"Jelly bean yourself!" muttered Sprout between his teeth.

He ate much less than usual but nobody noticed. His father just said, "Bad luck about the dinghy, old man," but his mother and Mrs. Chad merely agreed that they had always thought those things were dangerous. They were much more concerned with Tilly and Albina, whom they tried to stuff with more Swiss cheese sandwiches.

Mrs. Chad, now quite happy again, was full of the details of Albina's adventure. Sprout gathered that when the strangers had slammed the trunk shut and started the car, Albina had squeaked and yelled and banged — but the people simply thought there was something wrong with the springs. "Dopes" thought Sprout. Albina's voice was nothing like a car spring. He was also disgusted to notice that, now it was all over, Mrs. Chad seemed to look upon it as quite a joke.

"Come on, dear, have another ginger snap," she chortled. "Never mind your fillings!"

At last the Chads were packed off into their home-going bus, and Sprout's family went back for supper at Mrs. Lupin's.

The only person who seemed really horrified at Sprout's bad luck was Eileen. She knew there was something wrong as soon as she saw him put down his knife and fork with the third fish stick untouched.

His mother had to explain that he wasn't ill; just a bit upset.

"A *bit*!" Eileen burst out when she had heard the story. "A bit! I should think so, too. If it was me, I'd be tearing my hair out!" She looked at Sprout's hair as if it might fall off the top of his head at any minute.

"You mean to say you won it, and they *sunk* it?" she blazed. "That's murderous! Almost as bad as if you picked the Derby winner and somebody shot him a yard before the post!"

She was so indignant that even the Commander couldn't help overhearing.

"Scuttled her, did they?" he muttered into his moustache.

Sprout didn't hear this, but was very much surprised when the Commander patted his tuft on the way out of the dining room.

"Cheer up," said Raymond when he and Sprout were in bed.

"I've got half a bar of chocolate," he tried again.
Still silence.

"Milk and nut." No answer.

"I might even have a caramel in my jacket pocket.
You can have that, too, if you like."

Sprout grunted.

"Well, shall I get it?"

Chops looked up, but Sprout lay like a stone.

"Listen!" said Raymond desperately. "I can hear an
airplane! Maybe it's that helicopter! Shall we look and
see?"

"No," said Sprout.

Raymond sighed and went to sleep.

The next morning, at breakfast time, Sprout's father was wanted on the phone.

He came back to his cooling bacon with a broad smile.

"Well," he said, "I call that very nice. *Very* nice!"

"What?" asked Sprout. For a wild moment, he wondered if they had salvaged his dinghy after all.

"You have an invitation from the RAF! A man down at that helicopter base says he'll be glad to show you two boys around. Says they do sometimes have parties of kids down there, to let them see the works. I imagine he wants to make up for sinking your dinghy."

Sprout said nothing. There was nothing to say, if anybody could think they could make up for such a thing.

Eileen scuttled across with another plate full of toast.

"Some of it's brown," she apologized. "Commander Piper went off in such a hurry this morning, he left a couple of pieces. Not like him at all. Mrs. Lupin says he never even stopped to tap the barometer. I hope he's all right."

Sprout wasn't interested in either the Commander or brown toast.

All that morning on the beach, he was still gloomy. The sight of so many dinghies in the sea brought everything home to him again.

"Why don't you put your flippers on and go and have a swim?" said his father.

"Stupid things," muttered Sprout. "Tilly can have them."

"*Can* I?" Tilly beamed in amazement. "For all my own?"

"I said so, didn't I?" Sprout grunted. "And I hope they make you fall over!"

"Sprout, what a horrid thing to say!" protested his mother. She knew he was upset, but this was going too far.

"Sprout's cross!" Tilly announced radiantly. "But I'm not, so it doesn't matter. Not at *all*," she added, and held out her sandy toes for the flippers to be fastened on.

By lunchtime, Sprout's parents were both looking forward to the afternoon, when surely he would be distracted by going over to see the helicopter.

Eileen looked distracted at lunch, too — but in a different way.

"The Commander hasn't come in!" she said. "We can't understand it at all. He hasn't missed a meal in seven years, and he hasn't even given Mrs. Lupin so much as a call. She's close to calling the police!"

"I wouldn't worry," said Sprout's father.

"Mrs. Lupin's every bit as worried as I am!" Eileen retorted, slamming down the cheese.

Sprout was surprised. He had never seen Eileen upset before.

"Is Eileen cross, too?" Tilly asked.

"Not cross, bless you," said Eileen. "Only Mrs.

Lupin had saved him an extra thick piece of haddock.
And now it's dry as an old duster! — Well, isn't it to
be expected that she'd be disappointed?"

None of them said anything, but Sprout's father
gave his mother rather a quick look, which Sprout
took to mean that they both thought the same as he
did: that the Commander often got the best helpings.

At five to three Chops jumped out of the car,
looking happy; followed by Raymond, looking eager;
followed by Sprout, looking nothing in particular.
Reg, wearing a flying suit, was waiting for them. He
told Sprout's father that it would be all right to come
back for them in about an hour.

"— But, hey, don't forget the dog!" he called.

"That's Chops," said Sprout. "He wants to stay."

"Oh, he does, does he?" said Reg. "I said boys, not
dogs. We don't encourage dogs on the runway."
Then he looked at Sprout's face. "Oh. Well, all right,
as long as you keep him on a leash, and he behaves
himself. He'd better, if you don't want to lose him,
too!"

"What d'you mean?" said Sprout furiously.

"Keep your hat on, son, I was only joking,"
grinned Reg. "But you'll have to hold him well clear
when we start her up, or he'll wonder what's happen-
ing to his wool!"

Sprout saw what he meant, later on.

But first, with Chops held firmly on a short chain,
they did the rounds of the huts. Some of this, Sprout

thought, was rather boring. Bathrooms, laundry rooms, storerooms, walls covered with maps. The maps appealed to Raymond, who wanted to know what all the marks on them were for.

"Black circles for coast guard stations," said Reg, "circles with a cross in them for large hospitals, 'L' for lifeboat, 'Z' for Zodiac."

"What's that?" Raymond asked.

"The name for an inflatable raft. They're manned by the — hey, where's your pal off to?"

Sprout had taken Chops to the door. He did not want to hear about inflatable rafts.

"I thought we were going *inside* the helicopter," he said. After all, he had been in this hut yesterday; he was beginning to think he might just as well have stayed on the beach.

"So we are. Come on," said Reg. "Hey, Nobby!"

The stocky little winchman appeared from the next room and grinned cheerfully.

"Want me to put my gear on?" he asked. He unhooked an enormous yellow garment from the door.

"OK, see you out there," said Reg, leading the way toward one of the yellow machines.

"Now then, I don't know about that dog."

"He'll be good if I tell him to," said Sprout.

"Doesn't chew things up, does he?"

"Only bones," said Sprout. "He's not a puppy," he added scornfully.

"OK, OK, no offense. You keep tight hold of him, that's all."

One side of the helicopter was wide open. Sprout looked in and saw a dark space, rather like the hold of a very small ship, neatly stacked with strange things.

"Who's going first?" asked Reg, but he needn't have asked. Chops was up and over the edge before Sprout could even get his foot on the step.

"Good thing we're on the ground," said Reg cheerfully, hoisting Sprout's lower half into the aircraft.

"Well, you're a bit lighter," he remarked as he did the same for Raymond. "Wouldn't have to throw out much fuel for you!"

"What d'you mean, throw out fuel?" Sprout asked. For the first time, he was beginning to take an interest.

"The weight of a helicopter has to be exact," said Reg. "The fuel's gauged in pounds, so we have to throw out exactly the number of pounds to make up for the weight of the survivor."

"Did you have to throw out any for Tilly?" asked Sprout.

"Not as much as we would for you and wool-face there," Reg grinned. "Heaven help us if we had to pick up you two!"

"Where's the driver's seat?" asked Sprout.

"Pilot's, you mean," said Raymond scornfully.

"All right, who cares?" Sprout was beginning to feel cross again. But Reg cheerfully said he'd take

them up, one at a time, to the cockpit; the other one
would have to hold Chops.

So Sprout found himself sitting at the controls, with
an instrument panel and a sort of windshield in front,
and nothing at all at the sides.

"Aren't you afraid of falling out?" he asked, "when
you go all crooked?"

"Helicopters don't go crooked," said Reg. "They just go any way they like. Up, down, sideways, hover — that's the great thing about them. Anyway, try this."

He fastened Sprout into an enormous strap—then another, and another—and buckled him up tight.

"Now, then, you could be upside down and not fall out of that."

Sprout agreed; but the straps made him feel that perhaps he had had too much lunch after all, and Chops was whining down below.

"Are we going for a ride?" he asked. He remembered that Chops was not strapped in.

"Are you joking?" said Reg, amazed. "It'd be more than my job was worth! We're not allowed to take people for joyrides, you know. Besides, you haven't even got a life jacket on!"

"*He's* got something on," said Sprout. He was looking out of the open side at the approaching figure of Nobby. Or rather, at a figure that must be Nobby, because of the cheery red face sticking out of the top. Otherwise, it was more like something out of one of those space programs that Raymond liked so much: big black rubber boots at the bottom, a great yellow bagginess in the middle, and a shiny flying helmet tucked under one arm. Also, in the middle section, there appeared to be various gadgets attached: a strap over one shoulder, and things stuck into pockets on both sleeves. The only un-space-like thing was a rather battered box that Nobby carried in his free hand; it was labeled "Margarine."

"That's his winchman's outfit," said Reg.

"Hey!" Raymond called. "It's my turn to come up there!"

So Sprout changed places with him and took Chops to talk to Nobby.

"Why do you have to wear all that?" he asked.

"When you drop into the sea for a rescue," said Nobby, "there are a lot of things you might need. For instance, say it was at night. Well, in one of these pockets I've got a chemical that lights up the water. Makes it fluorescent — know what I mean?"

"Aren't you hot?" asked Sprout.

"You try dropping into the sea on a cold day, half a mile out . . . hold on, I think Reg wants me."

Reg was waving from the helicopter. Raymond and Chops jumped out of it.

"I imagine he's ready for the demonstration," said Nobby, lumbering across the field. He placed the margarine box on a patch of stubby grass in the middle.

From the huts another figure appeared, also equipped for action.

"Ginger said you wanted a navigator," he said.

"Right," said Reg. "Carry on."

The navigator climbed into the plane and began to

unwind a cable. Nobby was fastening himself into a thing made of huge canvas strips. His short legs stuck out of the lower strips, and his chest and shoulders out of the top strips.

"Bosun's chair," he explained. "See — I can move my arms and legs as much as I like. Free as a bird, you might say."

He looked like the bulkiest bird Sprout had ever seen.

"This is where the hook goes," he explained. The navigator attached a very large hook on the end of the cable to the front of Nobby's "chair."

"Right?" called Reg. "OK, you boys — stand well away. *And* dog. Better go over there in that long grass — see? Otherwise you'll be blown into kingdom come!"

The grass was tall and bleached; there were field poppies in it, and short, stubby, daisy-like flowers in bare patches close to the ground.

"Chamomile," said Sprout. Ever since he had won a potted plant competition at school, he had been keen on things that grow.

Suddenly, there was a hurricane.

At least, that was what it seemed in the first few seconds. There was a lot of noise, and violent wind.

The long grasses blew wildly and streamed flat; the poppies looked as if they wanted to fly for their lives; even the tough, stubby chamomile shook all over; and Chops's ears were like woolly pennants in a storm.

"He's started the engine!" shouted Raymond.

"I know!" Sprout shrieked back. It was as much as he could do even to shriek; the helicopter's whir was nearly blowing his tuft off.

"Look, they're up!" Raymond said. The grass and the poppies and Chops's ears subsided as the plane rose straight into the air.

"They've left that box behind," said Sprout. The margarine box looked tiny and forlorn, standing in the middle of the field.

"Silly, he's going to land on it," said Raymond.

"Who? How?"

"Just watch."

Sprout screwed up his eyes. All he could see was a blurred blob against the sky, but he realized that the blob was Nobby, and that he was being let down from a long way up. After a few moments' swaying about, he landed safely and neatly on the margarine box.

"Good shot!" said Raymond.

"I wish I could have a ride," said Sprout. "But I suppose they wouldn't let me."

He was quite right; they wouldn't.

"Couldn't I even just try on the uniform?" he asked when the demonstration was over.

Nobby looked at him, and looked at Reg, and they both grinned. Sprout's pink, disappointed face was more than they could resist.

"Be a bit big for you," said Nobby, "but I don't see

why not. Only we don't call it a uniform. And don't be surprised if you can't see out of the top!"

So he peeled off his winchman's outfit, and they lifted Sprout into it. He had certainly never worn anything so big or so stiff in his life. It was even bigger than the duffel coat his father had given him last Christmas. His eyes just peered over the collar, and his arms and legs were lost in balloons of bagginess. By the time they had strapped the life jacket on, there was hardly anything to be seen of him, except his tuft of hair at the top.

But he did manage to see over the edge enough to waddle a few steps in the great black boots. He beamed at Chops, who was looking very anxious.

"It's all right, Chops," he puffed. "I won't be a winchman really. But look at all my gadgets!" He flapped the sleeves; something near the end of one of them caught his eye.

"What's that?" he asked. It looked like the handle of a dagger, slotted into a flap.

"Oh, that's my razor," said Nobby. "Use it for slitting things. Like, say yesterday, when—"

"Get me out of this!" Sprout interrupted very loudly indeed. Even Chops looked taken aback.

"I don't want it on anymore," Sprout muttered, this time very quietly.

And he didn't say another word until his father came to take them home.

"Well, enjoy yourselves, did you?" he asked them in the car. "Had a good afternoon, eh?"

"Oh, yes!" said Raymond enthusiastically.

"No," said Sprout.

All the way back to Mrs. Lupin's, he thought about that razor. His father didn't know what was the matter. Raymond chattered on and on about smoke-floats, mini-flares, heliographs — he seemed to have become a mine of information and to have forgotten everything that had happened the day before. Sprout almost wished that they were really going home and not back to Mrs. Lupin's at all; it seemed hardly worth finishing the vacation.

His father was puzzled.

"I can't make him out," he said to Sprout's mother when they were changing for dinner. "They even let him put on some of their gear — you'd have thought that'd cheer him up. But he came home with a face like a rainy day."

"Never mind," sighed his mother. "Maybe there'll be baked potatoes. . . ."

There were (she had smelled them); but Sprout had hardly stuck a knife into his when Eileen rushed back into the dining room with her face shining and her eyes nearly popping out of her head.

"It's Commander Piper!" she squawked. "He's back!"

"Oh. Well, good," said Sprout's father vaguely.

"He wants to see you! He says he won't sit down to his dinner until you come!"

"Who — me?"

"No, no. Sprout! It's Sprout he wants!"

Sprout blinked.

"Yes, you, my rascal! He's out there in the hall, and I'm to keep his potato hot till he gives me the word. And he won't do that till you've . . . oh come along, do . . . and Mrs. Lupin's so pleased to see the face of the dear man again," she added with a great beam. "But do come quickly!"

Sprout looked at Eileen, and then at his potato. He stuck his fork into it like a mast.

"I've licked that fork," he told his family threateningly.

Eileen almost pushed him into the hall. He couldn't understand what she was so excited about; a private chat with Commander Piper wasn't *his* idea of fun.

But then his mouth dropped open.

His eyes went round as buttons.

His tuft stood on end.

There, in the middle of the hall, sat the Commander — in the biggest blown-up dinghy Sprout had ever seen! The Commander himself looked somewhat blown-up, too, because he was wearing a brand-new white life jacket. Above it, his face was pink, and his eyes sparkled with satisfaction.

"Got her this morning from Tubby Trotter's," he

said, patting the side of the dinghy. "Last one he had.
But the silly man had run out of life jackets, so I had
to go halfway across the county for these."

Sprout saw that there was another jacket, neatly
folded up, in the bottom of the boat.

"Well, no good giving you the boat without the
jackets, " the Commander went on. "Anybody who
doesn't wear these is a fool. Suicidal. Here, you'd
better try it on." He handed Sprout the second jacket.

"D'you mean it's for me?" Sprout gasped.

"Of course. What d'you suppose?" Commander
Piper said in his old snappy way. "Couldn't help
overhearing what had happened. Never like to think
of a man's ship being scuttled. It's bad luck. Anyway,
she'll take you and a crew of one. Oh, and there's a
rope, in case you want to tie her up. Which, if you
take the advice of an old sailor, you'll do."

Sprout saw a large coil of clean new rope lying on
Mrs. Lupin's hall rug.

He was speechless. The dinghy was bigger than his
prize one; it was bigger than any he had ever seen at
Seabay. Blown up, it almost filled the hall.

"Isn't it a whopper!" beamed Eileen.

"*She*," the Commander said.

"—And he says there's enough rope there for you
to go out for miles and still be safe!"

"A hundred yards," said the Commander. "But that
can seem a lot farther than you think, in a high wind.

And with a light craft like this. Better make sure your father knows how to tie her up."

"Jiminy!" said Sprout.

He couldn't think of anything else to say, except "Golly," or "Wow" — and none of these words could possibly tell what he felt. He had never been one for saying much, anyway; and besides, Eileen was pushing his arms through the holes of the life jacket.

Then Commander Piper heaved himself out of the dinghy, nearly bringing down the umbrella stand and a potted fern as he did so.

"Well, good sailing," he said briskly. He was not one for many words, either, but his eyes still sparkled, and Sprout's face meant more to him than any thanks.

"I'll make a flag" said Sprout, back at the dinner table. "And next time I see that helicopter, I'll wave to it. From the *sea*. And not because I want rescuing, either."

"What color flag?" asked Raymond.

"Any color," said Sprout. "But on it will be written PIPER. Because that's the name of my boat. *Piper!*" He raised his voice and looked radiantly across at the Commander, who was just being served by Mrs. Lupin in person.

The Commander nodded but seemed to be more interested in either Mrs. Lupin or his late dinner.

"I wonder if they make these for dogs," said Sprout. Chops had just put a paw on his knee, perhaps wondering why he looked a different shape. Certainly, the life jacket did keep Sprout rather far away from the potato, but that didn't matter.

After all, there couldn't be many people who were at that moment eating a baked potato in a life jacket.

Or who were so happy.